PLAYING
PRO
SPORTS

PLAYING PRO
BASKETBALL

Marty Gitlin

Ŀ Lerner Publications Company ● Minneapolis

Lerner Publications Company
A division of Lerner Publishing Group, Inc.
241 First Avenue North
Minneapolis, MN 55401 USA

For reading levels and more information, look up this title at
www.lernerbooks.com.

Content Consultant: Devean George, 11-year NBA veteran

Library of Congress Cataloging-in-Publication Data

Gitlin, Marty.
    Playing pro basketball / by Martin Gitlin.
       pages   cm. — (Playing pro sports)
    Includes index.
    ISBN 978–1–4677–3845–3 (lib. bdg. : alk. paper)
    ISBN 978–1–4677–4727–1 (eBook)
    1. Basketball—Juvenile literature. 2. Professional sports—
Juvenile literature. I. Title.
    GV885.1.B355 2015
    796.323—dc23   2013042394

Manufactured in the United States of America
1 – PC – 7/15/14

CONTENTS

CHAPTER ONE

WELCOME TO

The Miami Heat needed a miracle. It was June 18, 2013. Miami was facing the San Antonio Spurs in Game 6 of the National Basketball Association (NBA) Finals. The star-studded Heat had been favored to win. But the Spurs led 94–89 with just 23 seconds remaining. A Spurs win would clinch the championship.

Miami had relied on its three stars that season. Forward LeBron James was an all-around superstar. Guard Dwyane Wade scored lots of points from the backcourt. And center Chris Bosh was a force under the basket. Yet with the season on the line, Miami put forth a total team effort.

James missed a long jump shot with 23 seconds left. All seemed lost. But teammate Mike Miller was in position. He grabbed the rebound and passed the ball back to James. This time, James's three-point shot went in. The Spurs' lead was down to 94–92.

Miami Heat forward LeBron James shoots during Game 6 of the NBA Finals.

THE NBA

San Antonio added a free throw. Miami now trailed 95–92 with seven seconds left. Then James missed another three-point attempt. Again, all seemed lost. But again, Miami got another chance. Bosh grabbed the rebound. He then found guard Ray Allen in the corner.

Allen had been a star for many years in the NBA. By 2013 he was a veteran role player. His role for the Heat was to make three-point shots. And that is exactly what he did on this night. Allen sank a three-pointer to tie the game at 95–95.

That marked one of the fastest and greatest comebacks in league history. Soon the Heat were celebrating an overtime victory. And then the Heat went on to win Game 7. It marked their second straight NBA title. Miami's big three stars got much of the attention. However, the win was a total team effort. Without smart plays by reliable role players, Miami might have lost Game 6.

A Modest History

Basketball is a fast-paced game. Athleticism is key. Players must be able to move quickly down the court. Sharp cuts help players get open on offense. Great jumping ability and timing helps players grab rebounds or block shots. But basketball is also a very technical game.

The Heat's Ray Allen puts up his game-tying shot in Game 6 of

Players who reach the NBA need to have strong fundamentals and a well-rounded game. If a player excels only at shooting, for example, NBA defenders will focus on stopping that. The player must also be able

to dribble and pass well. Without great fitness, great fundamentals, and a well-rounded game, a player's NBA career is not likely to last long.

Basketball is one of the most popular sports in the United States. It is growing in popularity around the world. That has made the NBA ultracompetitive. It was not always that way, though.

Basketball began as a sport in the late 1800s. The sport was not very popular at first. Sports such as baseball and boxing took most of the attention. However, basketball was growing. One important step came in 1937. That was when the National Basketball League (NBL) was founded. It was one of the first professional basketball leagues.

The NBL began small. Its teams were based in mid-sized cities such as Akron, Ohio, and Sheboygan, Wisconsin. By 1946 a new league formed. It was called the Basketball Association of America (BAA). The BAA took the sport into bigger cities such as New York, New York, and Boston, Massachusetts. The leagues saw a bright future, so in 1949, the BAA and NBL combined. That created the NBA.

Quotable

"That was the way the game was played—get a lead and put the ball in the icebox. Teams literally started sitting on the ball in the third quarter."
—Hall of Fame point guard Bob Cousy about the slow pace of games before the NBA added a 24-second clock in 1954

Oklahoma City Thunder superstar Kevin Durant

Better Than Ever

The NBA has grown in popularity ever since. Each generation that followed had great teams and great players. First, it was the Minneapolis Lakers. They controlled the NBA in the 1950s. Then the Boston Celtics dominated the NBA in the 1960s. It was in the 1980s, however, that the NBA became hugely popular. Earvin "Magic" Johnson led the Los Angeles Lakers. Larry Bird led the Boston Celtics. Fans could not get enough of the rivalry between the two players and two teams. Then Michael Jordan and the Chicago Bulls dominated in the 1990s. All of those players and those teams helped make the NBA one of the most popular sports leagues in the world. And the league is still growing.

The growth has been great for fans. NBA games are fast-paced and exciting. However, competition for players

Superstitions

Athletes tend to be superstitious. They pay close attention to their routines. If a player performs well, he might try to mimic that routine before the next game. Jason Terry is a veteran point guard. For many years, Terry ate chicken fingers before each game. He stopped that tradition. However, he kept up his other pregame ritual. Terry owns shorts from every NBA team. Every night before a game, he sleeps in the shorts of the team he plays next. It seems to work. For example, Terry won an NBA title with the Dallas Mavericks in 2011.

is tougher than ever. The players who make it to the NBA have spent hours in the gym. They come into each season in top shape. They watch video and study the game. That is because the players know talent can get them only so far. Anything less than their best might not be good enough.

IN THE SPOTLIGHT

There has been little criticism of LeBron James since he entered the NBA in 2003. After all, he is considered one of the greatest players in the history of the sport. But some people claimed James did not use his incredible strength while close to the basket on offense. James did not post up enough. That requires fighting for position near the basket, accepting a pass, and using power and quickness to work for a shot.

The criticism continued after James's team, the Miami Heat, lost in the 2011 NBA Finals. So James decided to improve his post-up game. The Heat needed more inside scoring. James went to work out with former Houston Rockets star Hakeem Olajuwon. Olajuwon had been one of the best post-up players ever. Olajuwon taught James how to take advantage of a defender close to the basket. James used those new skills to help the Heat win the 2012 and 2013 NBA championships.

CHAPTER TWO

TAKING THAT

For many years, the best high school basketball players went to college before the NBA. They usually spent three or four years playing college ball. Then they entered the NBA Draft. By the 1990s, more and more players were going to college for only a year or two. And some players skipped college altogether. Superstars such as Kobe Bryant and Kevin Garnett were drafted out of high school. LeBron James graduated from high school in 2003. Soon after, he was the first overall pick in that year's NBA Draft.

Players can no longer follow that path, though. The NBA set an age limit in 2006. A player must now be 19 in the calendar year of the NBA Draft to be eligible. That means most players have to spend at least one year in college or playing overseas.

Kobe Bryant was only 18 when he debuted for the Los Angeles Lakers in 1996.

GIANT STEP

The move surprised some people. After all, Bryant, Garnett, and James had become huge stars. The league noticed another trend, though. Many players who were drafted out of high school struggled. There is already a big gap in play between the NBA and college basketball. The difference between high school and the NBA is even bigger. Some of the high school players were not physically ready for the NBA. Their bodies were less mature, and their basketball skills needed more work. Mental preparation

Portland Trail Blazers coach Nate McMillan, *front right*, directs center Greg Oden during a 2007 predraft workout.

was an issue too. Players were not prepared for the more complicated tactics. New players also have to adapt to the longer schedule. The NBA regular season is 82 games.

Some people disagreed with the age limit. But all incoming players must now abide by it. One benefit to the league is that all incoming players now have more experience. Before, scouts had to sometimes evaluate players based on their performance in high school. Now all incoming players have experience against higher-level competition. A few top high school players have since gone overseas to play professionally. However, most top North American players get that experience in college.

NBA scouts look at many factors in incoming players. Physical skills and talent are a given. However, scouts also look at the mental part of the game. Does a player make good decisions on the court? Does the player get along well with teammates and coaches? How does the player react to tough situations? Most importantly,

AAU

Most young basketball players suit up for their high school or prep school team. Many top young players also play for Amateur Athletic Union (AAU) teams. AAU teams are made up of players from several different schools. These teams play in games and tournaments around the country. The level of play is very high. College coaches are often seen scouting players at AAU tournaments. Many NBA players know one another from AAU tournaments growing up. AAU has its downfalls, though. Sometimes adults try to take advantage of top players. The adults try to influence the players to go to certain colleges or to align with certain companies.

how does a player compare against top competition? Scouts watch how these players defend, dribble, rebound, and shoot. They take notes about each player's fitness. Basketball is a grueling game. A player must be in great shape to last an entire 82-game season.

Excelling in college does not guarantee an NBA career. Every March, 68 college teams compete in the national championship tournament. A few weeks after that, just 60 players are taken in the NBA Draft. And only the first 30 have guaranteed roster spots. With basketball's global growth, many top players come from overseas. So only the most talented and well-prepared college players get taken.

Quotable

"For me, flexibility is huge. Staying loose and healthy and staying limber—you can tell a difference when your muscles are tight or when you're stretched out and completely relaxed."

—Los Angeles Clippers forward Blake Griffin on yoga. Yoga has become a popular training method for NBA players in recent years. Yoga poses help with relaxation, stretching, and strength.

Playing Strong

Power training is important to those seeking an NBA career. The key is finding a balance. NBA players need to be both strong and fast. Bulking up too much can rob a player of his quickness. But a player without enough bulk can get pushed around. The ideal player is tough and steady. He can get up and down the court quickly. And he is explosive when cutting or leaping.

Being a powerful player does not necessarily mean being big. Mike Brungardt served for 17 years as the San Antonio Spurs' strength and conditioning coach. He looks at more than a player's body. Brungardt attended the 2013 Portsmouth Invitational Tournament. That event features many of the top college prospects. Scouts from around the world attend. While there, Brungardt wrote a blog post:

Oklahoma City Thunder forward Kevin Durant dribbles against the Miami Heat in 2012.

A few years ago everyone was commenting on how weak [Oklahoma City Thunder superstar] Kevin Durant was based on his poor performance on the bench press at the Chicago [tryout]. The truth of the matter is you don't play basketball on your back pushing people off of you. You play

Chicago Bulls point guard Derrick Rose, *right*, dives for a loose ball against Miami Heat forward LeBron James.

on your feet, which means your core [hips, glutes, and abs] are the main determining factor in how strong you play.

Strength, speed, and quickness are key for NBA prospects. And all of those can be improved through training. However, some physical advantages cannot be improved. For example, height is important in basketball. Many NBA centers are around 7 feet (2.13 meters) tall. But even most guards are well over 6 feet (1.83 m) tall. Scouts also measure other parts of the body. They have players stand with their arms straight out to each side. The measurement from fingertip to fingertip is called wingspan. Players with long wingspans can play like they are taller. These players can cover more space on defense. However, undersized players can still make it in the NBA. The key, Brungardt wrote, is good speed, quickness, and agility:

Speed allows you to play aggressive defense. It gets you to the loose balls. It gives you the step to get by a defender. It gives you the step to cut off a penetrator. It beats your opponent to the other end [of the court] for the fast break. It gets you back to defend against the fast break. It leaves your defender in the dust on a back cut [to the basket]. With speed you can often overcome a mistake by getting

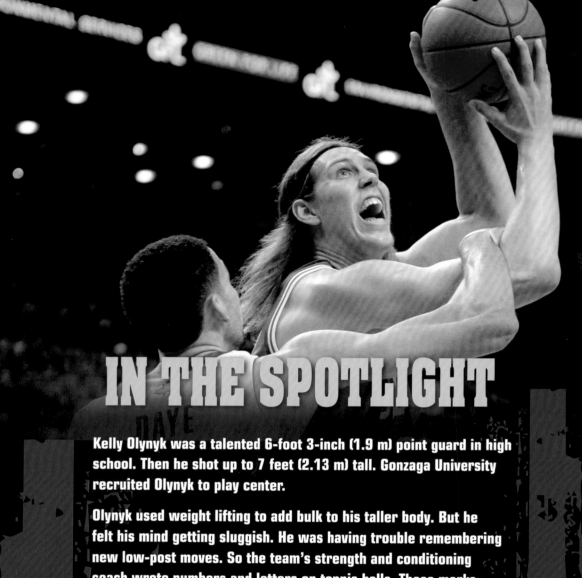

IN THE SPOTLIGHT

Kelly Olynyk was a talented 6-foot 3-inch (1.9 m) point guard in high school. Then he shot up to 7 feet (2.13 m) tall. Gonzaga University recruited Olynyk to play center.

Olynyk used weight lifting to add bulk to his taller body. But he felt his mind getting sluggish. He was having trouble remembering new low-post moves. So the team's strength and conditioning coach wrote numbers and letters on tennis balls. Those marks represented a movement on the court. The trainer then tossed the balls at Olynyk for a half hour every day. Olynyk would then catch the ball and perform the corresponding movement.

The goal was to get Olynyk to make those moves without thinking about them. The NBA game moves much faster than play at the college level. The tennis ball drill helped Olynyk grasp plays quicker and slow the game down in his mind. Olynyk was taken in the 2013 NBA Draft. He plays for the Boston Celtics.

yourself back in the play. Without it, you have to play perfect position all the time. There is no margin for error.

Speed and quickness can be improved through weight training and agility drills. The players who make it in the NBA are those who are both gifted basketball players and willing to put in the work to perform at their best.

CHAPTER THREE

STAYING HEALTHY,

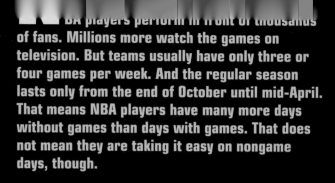

NBA players perform in front of thousands of fans. Millions more watch the games on television. But teams usually have only three or four games per week. And the regular season lasts only from the end of October until mid-April. That means NBA players have many more days without games than days with games. That does not mean they are taking it easy on nongame days, though.

The off-season is a time for players to refresh and prepare for the next season. For most NBA players, the off-season is also a time of hard work. Maintaining and improving fitness is essential. The off-season is also an ideal time to improve parts of one's game. For example, a player might work on adjusting the technique on his shot. Improving individual skills can be harder during the season. Players also have to focus on games, team strategy, scouting, and resting during the season.

Jason Kidd, then with the Phoenix Suns, looks through pregame notes by his locker before a 2001 game.

TAYING STRONG

Amar'e Stoudemire joined the NBA as a 19-year-old in 2002. He made six All-Star teams through the 2012–2013 season. Stoudemire explained his off-season program in an article for the Stronger Team website.

After waking up at eight o'clock in the morning, Stoudemire said he eats breakfast that usually consists of granola or fruit. After that, he does stretching exercises and some strength training. He follows that with work on his basketball skills. Stoudemire might start by working on different kinds of shots. Then he will work on other skills, such as offensive moves and ball handling. He said he usually wraps up around noon.

Stoudemire follows his schedule five or six days per week. But he

New York Knicks center Amar'e Stoudemire dunks the ball in 2013.

does not play in 5-on-5 games during the off-season. He said he concentrates only on personal development.

Players get into top shape as the season goes on. But they must be prepared to start the preseason in good shape. Training camp begins in early October. The preseason exhibition games begin about one week later. By that time, players have established an in-season workout routine.

Workout routines might differ depending on the player. Kobe Bryant said he tries to come into the season in top shape. Then, during the season, he focuses on basketball skills and building his endurance. He estimates that he takes between 700 and 1,000 practice shots every day. Bryant also lifts weights to build upper body strength. His goal is to get stronger and stronger as the season goes on.

Bryant's training routine has helped make him one of

The Rookie Wall

Some NBA rookies burst onto the scene with great play. NBA veterans know what is coming, though: the rookie wall. Most rookies experience the wall. It often occurs sometime around the middle of their first season. The player starts feeling exhausted and sluggish. His performance on the court usually slips. Mistakes are more common. The rookie wall is often unavoidable. The NBA season is more than twice as long as a college season. NBA games are eight minutes longer than college games. And NBA teams usually play more games per week than college teams. Some rookies just need some extra rest and then regain their form. Sometimes, however, rookies just have to play through the wall and build up their fitness for the next season.

the fittest players in the NBA. That is important, because he plays a lot of minutes. In his first 17 seasons, Bryant averaged more than 36 minutes per game. Few players see that much court time. Some players are lucky to get into a game for five minutes. Those bench players still have to remain fit, though. Sometimes those players will lift weights or do a cardio session after a game.

Lifting weights during the NBA season was once frowned upon. Today it is a common practice. Denver Nuggets team physician Steven M. Traina explained the growing practice of in-season weight lifting:

People used to think in basketball that if you lifted weights, you couldn't shoot because you're too muscle-bound. These guys spend a lot of time in the weight room. You look at the athletes now compared to 20 or 25 years ago, and they're cut, they're muscular.

Snoozing before Dribbling

In the afternoon before an evening game, many NBA players can be found napping. This has become an important part of the routine for many players. NBA players often have uneven sleep schedules. They are often out past midnight on nights when they have a game. Then they have to wake up early for practice or other commitments. Constant travel can take a toll as well. Athletes perform better when they are well rested. Napping gives players more focus and energy for the evening's game. Some players say napping also helps relieve boredom. Players often have many hours to kill in the afternoons before games.

Daily Grind

Half of an NBA regular season is played on the road. That means players are frequently on the move from city to city. Between all the games and the travel, players still

A trainer stretches Dallas Mavericks forward Shawn Marion before a 2009 game.

have lots of commitments. A full day off from games, practicing, or other obligations is rare during the season.

Game day for players usually starts in the morning. The players come in to the arena for a casual practice called a shootaround. This usually lasts approximately one hour. It is a time when the players take lots of practice shots. The players also go over strategies for that day's game. Coaches and players study their opponents' strengths and weaknesses throughout the week. Teams go over some of that information during the morning shootaround. Another benefit of the shootaround is getting the players' bodies moving. Players spend many hours on airplanes and buses. Sleep is not always regular. The morning shootaround is an opportunity to loosen up.

After the shootaround, players split up. Some go

Quotable

"Our nickname for him is 'Every day Ray.' It's every day. It's not every other day. It's not some days. It's every single day Ray. His work ethic and his discipline are in the top percentage in this league. Ninety-nine percent of the players do not have that type of consistent work ethic."
—Miami Heat coach Erik Spoelstra on veteran shooting guard Ray Allen. Allen arrives at games three and a half hours early to take extra shooting practice. That dedication helped him become the NBA's all-time leader in three-pointers.

Oklahoma City Thunder point guard Russell Westbrook warms up before a game in the 2012 NBA Finals.

home or back to the hotel to prepare for the game. Others might meet with an athletic trainer to stretch or treat a nagging injury. For the most part, though, players spend the next several hours resting.

Los Angeles Lakers forward Pau Gasol talks with a reporter in 2013.

Players are usually expected back at the arena 90 minutes before tip-off. Athletic trainers are waiting to help get the players ready. Some players need to stabilize their ankles with tape or braces. Members of the press are briefly allowed into the locker room for questions. Coaches will work with the players to review scouting reports about the opponent. For the most part, though, players spend that time getting ready for the game.

After the game, players return to the locker room to change. Members of the media are allowed back into the locker room at this time for more questions. The postgame routine differs for each player. Some simply shower, get dressed, and leave. Others might head to the weight room for another workout. Many players also receive treatment at this time. Persistent injuries are common during a long NBA season.

Eventually, the players head back home or to the team's hotel. Visiting teams sometimes go straight to the airport to get a head start home or to the next city. The hectic schedules sometimes make it hard for players to get sleep. Players might need several hours to wind down from a game too. That means they do not go to bed until the early hours of the morning. Eventually they have to sleep, though, because they most likely have another practice or game the next day.

Body Care

The NBA season is long and trying. Good nutrition habits keep players going strong throughout. NBA players are

Dwyane Wade, *right*, of the Miami Heat passes to a teammate during a 2013 game.

very active. They require protein-rich diets and lots of carbohydrates to stay strong and energized. Most NBA players avoid fatty foods or foods with lots of sugar or sodium. Drinking plenty of water is important too.

Unlike practice, however, nutrition is mostly up to the player. Trainers can recommend a diet. Only the player can follow through with it, though. Many veteran players credit nutrition with helping their bodies hold up. Dwyane Wade was a star pretty quickly after entering the NBA in 2003. At the time, he got away with eating fatty foods such as chicken fingers and cheeseburgers. He still ate those foods when his team, the Miami Heat, won the 2006 NBA title. But Wade noticed his body changing as he got older. He no longer had as much energy. So he focused on a more nutrient-rich diet. Gone are the fatty and salty foods. Now Wade focuses on fruits, salads, and juices.

Wade does not particularly like vegetables. So instead of eating straight veggies, he often mixes them into juice. Wade works with a nutritionist who helps determine a healthful meal plan. The nutritionist said Wade's postgame meal is one of the most important. That is because Wade loses approximately 5 pounds (2.27 kilograms) per game. He usually regains that weight by eating a simple meal based around a lean protein, such as a chicken or turkey breast.

Taking care of one's body goes beyond nutrition. NBA players put a lot of strain on their bodies. Stretching and sports massages help keep the body from breaking down. Many players also sit in ice baths after a game or an intense workout. Ice baths help relieve pain and speed up recovery from injuries. However, without proper supervision, ice baths can be dangerous. The cold water can send the body into shock.

IN THE SPOTLIGHT

NBA All-Star Andre Iguodala does not sleep in and take it easy during the off-season. He does not change his eating habits, either. Players usually lose some fitness during the off-season. But Iguodala makes an effort to stay in good shape year-round.

Iguodala usually wakes up around 8:30 a.m. After that, he has a light breakfast. Then he starts his first workout at 10 a.m. Iguodala often uses this time to work on improving basketball skills, such as dribbling with his off-hand. After that, he does a series of stretches. That is followed by 90 minutes of shooting drills. His goal is to make at least 500 baskets. His day ends with weight lifting. He works out a different group of muscles each day.

This off-season routine has worked well for Iguodala. He played in at least 80 games six times in his first nine seasons.

CHAPTER FOUR

GETTING INJURED,

Other sports have more collisions than basketball. No other sport has more injuries than basketball, though. The US Consumer Product Safety Commission (CPSC) reviewed injury information from different sports. It found that nearly 1.5 million basketball injuries were reported in 2011. The CPSC noted that the number of total injuries was likely higher because not all injuries were reported.

Body contact causes some injuries in basketball. Many injuries also come from the sharp movements. Players cut sharply as they dribble to the basket or move around on defense. Or sometimes players land awkwardly or on another player's foot when jumping. These types of movements can result in sprained ankles. Sprained ankles are the most common injuries among NBA players.

A sprained ankle can limit a player's ability to move. Continuing to play on a sprained ankle can cause even more damage to the knees, hips, and lower back. Players who sprain an ankle often have to take at least a few days off. Sprained ankles can be treated by icing the ankle or through anti-inflammatory drugs. However, the only way to truly recover is by resting.

The Chicago Bulls' Joakim Noah, center, and the Utah Jazz's Al Jefferson, left, get physical under the basket during a 2013 game.

PLAYING HURT

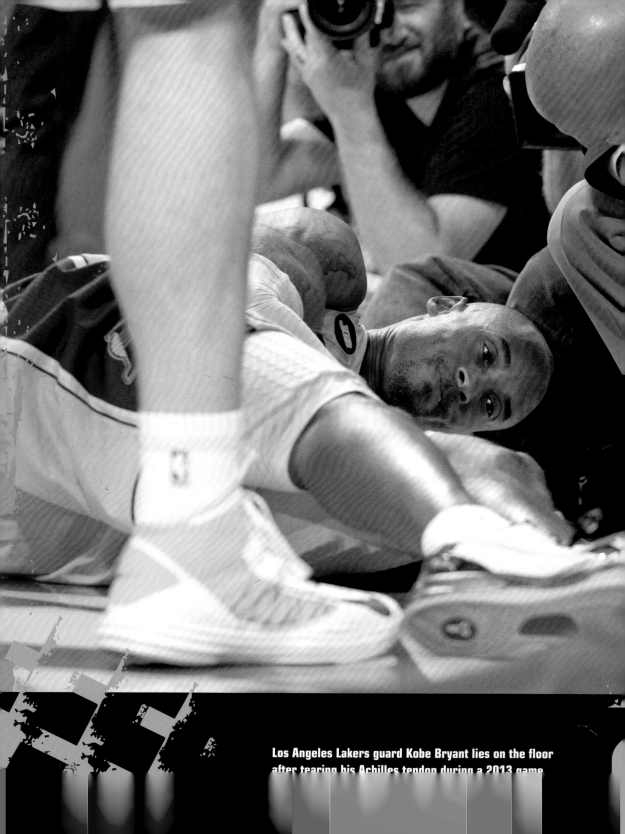

Los Angeles Lakers guard Kobe Bryant lies on the floor after tearing his Achilles tendon during a 2013 game.

Overuse injuries are common in basketball as well. These injuries occur due to repeated use of the same joints or body parts. Without enough time for rest and recovery, the body breaks down. This can lead to injuries such as tendinitis or stress fractures. Players who suffer from these injuries usually need to sit out until they recover.

Jumping is among the most common movements for NBA players. However, frequent jumping can lead to an overuse injury called jumper's knee. This occurs when the tendon in the knee becomes inflamed. The injury results in a constant throbbing pain just below the knee. Many players try to play through jumper's knee. But doing this can often make the problem worse. Players who recognize and treat the injury early can avoid serious damage.

Achilles tendinitis is another overuse injury.

Injuries: The Center of Attention

The NBA participated in a 17-year study of injuries beginning in 1992. Trainers from each team submitted information about the injuries their players suffered. The idea was to determine the injury patterns and medical conditions of players in the league. A total of 1,094 players were placed in the database. The league learned that ankle sprains were the most common injuries. They made up 13.2 percent of all injuries. But the study also revealed that knee inflammation caused players to miss the most games.

This is a strain or tear of the tendon that connects the calf to the heel. A torn rotator cuff is another overuse injury. The rotator cuff is an area of the shoulder that can be overworked by constant shooting and rebounding.

Dealing with injuries can be a struggle for some NBA players. Competition for playing time is fierce. Sometimes players worry that taking time off to treat an injury might result in less playing time when they return. Professional athletes also tend to be very competitive. Either way, players sometimes try to play through minor injuries. But doing so can result in worse problems down the road.

Traumatic Injuries

Basketball was originally considered a noncontact sport. But watching one minute of a modern NBA game can tell a viewer that there is plenty of contact today. Bodies often crash into one another, leading to hard falls to the hard floor. The result can be a traumatic injury. These are injuries such as broken bones or concussions.

A traumatic injury can occur at any time in an NBA game. Every team must employ an experienced medical staff. These people are prepared to immediately treat any injury that arises during a game or practice. Their expertise and quick response time helps serious injuries from becoming even worse. That showed on February 26, 2007.

The Los Angeles Clippers were playing the Charlotte Bobcats that day. In the first quarter, Clippers guard Shaun Livingston scooped up a loose ball. He then drove to the basket and attempted a layup. He missed the layup. Even worse, Livingston landed awkwardly on his left foot. He immediately screamed in pain. On such a simple play, he had dislocated his left kneecap.

The fans in the arena fell silent. Livingston's knee was twisted at an odd angle. Team doctor Steven Shimoyama raced out to Livingston. The doctor decided to pop the knee back into place. It was a risky decision. If the first attempt did not work, a second attempt would have

Los Angeles Clippers guard Shaun Livingston is taken off the court on a stretcher after injuring his knee against the Charlotte Bobcats in 2007.

an even smaller chance of success. But the doctor knew that the dislocation was cutting off blood circulation to Livingston's foot. That could have led to worse problems.

Failure to solve the problem could mean that Livingston's lower leg would have to be amputated.

Shimoyama flexed the injured knee and hip to loosen the hamstring. He placed his elbow on the knee and popped it back into place. Livingston described the injury and the treatment that might have saved his career. He said:

My leg was crooked. It was like this part was this way and my kneecap was like behind my knee. It's almost like popping a shoulder, popping a finger back into place, but it's a knee. He did that probably within the first 10 or 15 seconds. That was the most agonizing pain ever.

Preventing Injuries

Team doctors can treat injuries as soon as they happen. Players can also take steps to prevent injuries from

Dallas Mavericks players warm up before a 2009 game.

happening in the first place. Of course, some injuries are unavoidable. A player who goes up for a rebound might land on someone's foot and sprain an ankle. There is no way to avoid that. But some simple steps can help avoid other injuries.

For example, there are many ways that players can lower their chances of getting a sprained ankle. Many of them are easy. Simply warming up helps the body prepare for full-speed action. This includes stretching. Players who routinely stretch and have more flexibility are less likely to get injured. Equipment plays a role as well. NBA players often wear shoes that give more support to their ankles. It is also important that their shoes stick well to the floor. In addition, players can do special exercises to strengthen their ankles.

IN THE SPOTLIGHT

Tim Grover is a famous trainer who owns Attack Athletics. Grover gave his business that name because he has his athletes attack their workouts. Athletes seeking the most grueling workouts often go to Grover. One of those athletes is veteran NBA forward Corey Maggette.

Maggette starts by completing a set of dumbbell grabs. Those involve running 20 dashes of 100 yards (91 m) while carrying weights. The weights increase by 5 pounds (2.27 kg) every time. Maggette then does a 100-yard bear crawl. That means he is running on all fours. He follows that with two fireman-carry drills. Those involve him finishing a set of 50-yard (46 m) runs while carrying a grown man.

Even that does not end the workout. The brutal sessions are not over until Maggette lifts stones, buckets, and ship anchors onto boxes. The boxes are placed higher and higher each time, from 2 to 6 feet (0.6 to 1.8 m).

CHAPTER FIVE

LEADER OF

Basketball has three basic positions. They are guards, forwards, and centers. Within each position are more specialties. For example, power forwards are generally taller and play closer to the basket. Small forwards are more known for their shooting, athleticism, defense, or all three. In today's NBA, teams use many different combinations. Some thrive with the traditional lineup of two guards, two forwards, and a center. But some teams now use three guards or a lineup with no center.

Regardless of the lineup, all teams use a point guard. The point guard is a team's main ball handler. The point guard brings the ball up the court on most possessions. He directs the defense and calls plays. Often the point guard sets the tempo for the entire offense.

Los Angeles Clippers point guard Chris Paul, left, drives against the Memphis Grizzlies in 2013.

THE COURT

That hardly means all point guards are the same, though. Jason Kidd was one of the NBA's best point guards from 1994 to 2013. He was one of the league's best passers and defenders. His skills helped make his teammates better. Yet Kidd averaged only 12.6 points per game. Stephen Curry is one of the NBA's top point guards today. His game is very different from Kidd's. Curry thrives for the Golden State Warriors by scoring lots of points. He scored 22.9 points per game in 2012–2013.

The best point guards make their teammates better. Shoot-first point guards such as Curry, Kyrie Irving, and Russell Westbrook can score a lot of points. That means opposing defenders have to pay

Los Angeles Lakers point guard Steve Nash is known for leading a fast-paced offense.

extra attention to these point guards. That tight defense might leave open space for the point guard to drive. Or it might leave a teammate open for a pass.

Pass-first point guards such as Kidd and Ricky Rubio do not score as many points. They make their impact by helping teammates score. Rubio can draw extra defenders with his dribble drives. Then he sends a pass to a wide-open teammate for an easy bucket. Rubio is known for his court vision. He can see how plays will develop before others. Rubio's vision and passing help make his entire Minnesota Timberwolves team harder to guard.

The best point guards can combine both passing and shooting. Steve Nash was a two-time Most Valuable Player (MVP) with the Phoenix Suns. At his peak, he was able to bring the ball up the court and direct a fast-moving offense.

The Point Forward

Traditional basketball positions have changed as the game has grown. Point guards are traditionally shorter players with great ball skills. However, some taller players have shown excellent ball skills as well. At times, teams have allowed these taller players to be the primary ball handler. They bring the ball up the court and guide the offense. This role has become known as the point forward. Point forwards are usually very athletic and are taller than point guards. That can make them a nightmare to match up against. Los Angeles Lakers great Earvin "Magic" Johnson was 6 feet 9 inches (2.06 m). However, he often played at the point during the 1980s. Today, Miami Heat superstar LeBron James sometimes plays the role of point forward. He is 6 feet 8 inches (2.03 m).

Jeremy Lin leads the Houston Rockets' offense during

Nash was particularly skilled at dishing the ball off while sprinting to the basket on a dribble drive. Nash fooled defenders with no-look passes. But he also tormented defenses with his ability to make three-pointers. That combination made him one of the best offensive point guards of his generation.

Chris Paul, Derrick Rose, and Rajon Rondo are among the next generation of top point guards. All three players excel at passing, dribbling, and scoring. They lead their offenses with precision. All three are also shutdown defenders. Limiting an opposing point guard is a good way to limit an opposing offense. As many of today's point guards are well over 6 feet (1.83 m) tall, some can even defend against bigger guards or forwards.

All Defense, No Offense

Ben Wallace never averaged more than 9.7 points per game in a season. He never had good moves under the basket. And he made just 41 percent of his free throws. That was among the worst percentages of any regular NBA player ever. Yet the 6-foot 10-inch (2.08 m) center was a standout in the league for 16 seasons. He even earned four All-Star Game selections. Wallace starred because of his defense. He could block shots and shut down almost anyone. Wallace won the Defensive Player of the Year Award four times in one five-year span. His story reflects the importance of defense in the NBA.

Setting the Tone

NBA offenses are generally defined by pace. That is why the point guard is so important. The point guard sets the pace for most teams. His speed, quickness, and skill

Dallas Mavericks power forward Dirk Nowitzki, *right*, is known for his great jump shot.

set helps determine the pace of an offense. Teams with younger, quicker point guards often run a fast-break offense. Those offenses start with a rebound. Next comes an outlet pass to the point guard. Then the possessions end with a drive to the basket for two points or an open three-pointer. Older or slower point guards generally run a half-court offense. These offenses emphasize player movement with and without the ball, sharp passing, and accurate outside shooting.

Some of the greatest point guards in the NBA have played for mediocre teams. Oscar Robertson is considered one of the greatest players ever. But his Cincinnati Royals of the 1960s were never able to reach the NBA Finals. And some of the greatest teams in NBA history did not rely on point guard play. For example, the Los Angeles Lakers won three NBA titles in a row from 2000 to 2002 without a dominant point guard.

That is because there is more than one way for players and teams to play. There are players who thrive in the NBA with unique styles. Dirk Nowitzki is one of the NBA's best power forwards. Yet he is known as much for his three-point shooting as he is for his play under the basket.

Quotable

"If you're trying to achieve, there will be no roadblocks. I've had them; everybody has had them. But obstacles don't have to stop you. If you run into a wall, don't turn around and give up. Figure out how to climb it, go through it, or work around it."
—Michael Jordan, who many believe to be the greatest NBA player of all time

IN THE SPOTLIGHT

The center is often the tallest player on a team. He usually positions himself under the basket. For many years, the position was defined by power and force. Kareem Abdul-Jabbar changed that. He entered the NBA in 1969. Abdul-Jabbar was graceful and fluid on the court. He scored more points than any player in NBA history. And he did so by often using his signature skyhook. Opponents could not defend against the high, arcing shot. To make the shot, Abdul-Jabbar hooked his arm in a roundabout motion while shooting the ball from the tips of his fingers. He stood at 7 feet 2 inches (2.18 m). He released the ball on the skyhook even higher. That made it nearly impossible to block.

Abdul-Jabbar mastered the skyhook in college. He used the skyhook often because dunking was banned at the time. The shot helped him win six NBA championships and three college championships.

Many players enter the NBA Draft each year. Only a few from each draft ever become All-Stars, though. The key to thriving in the NBA is teamwork. The league is filled with athletic and talented players. The players who win the most are often the ones who play well with their teammates. No one player can win a game. Most championship teams need two or three great scorers. Their entire lineup usually plays tough defense. And often they have a good point guard running the show.

Train Like a Pro

NBA players do all kinds of workouts throughout a season. Some focus on fitness. Others focus on basketball skills. For most NBA players, though, the most frequent training activity is shooting. Most NBA players take hundreds of practice shots every day. There is a difference between shooting and effectively shooting. Players practice effectively shooting by trying to mimic game speed and situations. J. J. Redick is one of the NBA's most dangerous jump shooters. He practices jump shots using a catch-and-shoot drill.

The drill includes two partners. One partner stands in the low post around the edge of the lane. Another partner stands at the top of the key. Redick starts the drill under the basket. Then he runs around the low-post partner and receives a pass from the partner on the key. Redick then stops and shoots right away or else takes a quick dribble first. After the shot, he runs back under the hoop and gets ready to go again. He does this five times from each side of the basket.

Redick receives the pass at a slightly different location every time. This helps him practice shots from different angles. The high tempo of this drill helps mimic a game situation. Redick has to move and react quickly. He also has to work through fatigue.

Basketball Gear Diagram

Uniform

Players on each team must all wear matching sleeveless tops and shorts.

Sleeve

Shooting sleeves are mostly a fashion statement. However, some players claim the sleeves improve blood circulation. Other fashion accessories include headbands and wristbands.

Kneepads

More and more NBA players are wearing extra pads on their knees and elbows. These pads help prevent injuries but sometimes limit a player's movement.

Shoes

Most NBA players wear high-top shoes to help stabilize their ankles.

Glossary

athleticism: the use of physical skills or capabilities

concussion: a brain injury that occurs when something jolts a person's head

draft: a system by which teams in a league select incoming talent

endurance: the ability to perform for an extended period

exhibition: a game that does not count in the standings

injury: a physical problem that often prevents a player from competing

nutritionist: an expert in nutrition

off-season: the time of year when a league is inactive

overtime: an extra period played to decide the winner of a tie game

prospect: a player with potential to compete in the NBA

rebound: securing a missed shot in basketball

scout: a person who seeks out talent for a professional team

superstition: an irrational belief or practice

veteran: a player who has lots of experience

For More Information

Hill, Anne E. *LeBron James: King of Shots*. Minneapolis: Twenty-First Century Books, 2013.
This book tells the story of LeBron James, who has been one of the NBA's most exciting players since entering the league in 2003.

Hoops Hype
http://www.hoopshype.com
This site is loaded with information and news about NBA teams and players.

NBA Hoop Troop
http://www.nbahooptroop.com
Visit this fun site for games, videos, and other information about the NBA.

Phelps, Richard "Digger." With John Walters and Tim Bourret. *Basketball for Dummies*. Hoboken, NJ: Wiley, 2011.
This book breaks down all aspects of basketball, from rules and regulations to information about the NBA and other basketball leagues.

Savage, Jeff. *Kevin Durant*. Minneapolis: Lerner Publications, 2012.
This book tells the story of Kevin Durant, one of the NBA's most prolific scorers.

SI Kids
http://www.sikids.com
The *Sports Illustrated Kids* website covers all sports, including basketball.

Source Notes

9   "History of the Shot Clock," *NBA*, October 22, 2001, http://www
    .nba.com/analysis/00422949.html.

18 Ryan Wood, "NBA Players Finding Benefits in Yoga," *USA
    Basketball*, accessed January 14, 2014, http://youth.usab.com
    /training-room/player-psychology/NBA-Players-Finding-Benefits-in
    -Yoga.htm.

19, 21 Mike Brungardt, "Looking for the NBA Body," *Portsmouth
    Invitational Tournament*, January 14, 2014, https://www
    .portsmouthinvitational.com/LOOKING_FOR_THE_NBA_BODY
    .html.

21, 23 Ibid.

28 Brandon Guarneri, "Kobe Bryant," *Men's Fitness*, January 14,
    2014, http://www.mensfitness.com/leisure/entertainment/kobe
    -bryant.

30 Chris Tomasson, "For Ray Allen, Steady Shooting Comes from
    Early Workouts," *Fox Sports Florida*, June 2, 2013, http://www
    .foxsportsflorida.com/nba/miami-heat/story/For-Ray-Allensteady
    -shooting-comes-from?%20blockID=907933&feedID=3720.

44 Jonathan Abrams, "Like Magic," *Grantland*, February 11, 2013,
    http://www.grantland.com/story/_/id/8934761/on-career
    -shaunlivingston-survived-one-worst-injuries-nba-history.

44 Matt Moore, "Derrick Rose Says His Injury Forced Him to Be
    'Selfish' Last Year," *CBSSports.com*, July 4, 2013, http://www
    .cbssports.com/nba/eye-on-basketball/22628655/derrickrose-
    says-that-his-injury-forced-him-to-be-selfish-last-year.

55 T. J. Allan, "How Michael Jordan's Mindset Made Him Great," *USA
    Basketball*, January 14, 2014, http://youth.usab.com
    /training-room/player-psychology/How-Michael-Jordan-s-Mindset
    -Made-Him-Great.htm?cmp=273&memberid=%5Bmemberid
    %5D&lyrisid=%5Boutmail.messageid%5D.

Index

About the Author

Marty Gitlin is a freelance writer based in Cleveland, Ohio. He has written more than 75 educational books, many about the world of sports, including histories of several NBA teams and biographies of NBA players. Gitlin has won more than 45 awards during his 25 years as a writer, including first place for general excellence from the Associated Press. He lives with his wife and three children in Ohio.

Photo Acknowledgments

The images in this book are used with the permission of: © Darrell Walker/Icon SMI, pp. 3 (top), 10–11; © Zuma Press/Icon SMI, pp. 3 (middle), 4–5, 6–7, 13, 19, 20–21, 32, 34–35, 37, 48–49, 52–53, 56; © Chris Keane/Icon SMI, pp. 3 (bottom), 47, 50; © Harris & Ewing/Library of Congress, p. 8; © John McDonough/Icon SMI, pp. 14–15, 24–25; © Richard Clement/Icon SMI, p. 16; © The Canadian Press, Frank Gunn/AP Images, p. 22; © Mark Goldman/Icon SMI, p. 26; © Icon SMI, p. 29; © Mark Halmas/Icon SMI, pp. 30–31; © Rick Bowmer/AP Images, pp. 38–39; © Icon SMI, pp. 40–41; © Chris Pizzello/AP Images, p. 43; © Albert Pena/Icon SMI, pp. 44–45, 54; © Mayskyphoto/Shutterstock Images, p. 59.

Front cover: © Jared Wickerham/Getty Images; © Valentina Razumova/Shutterstock.com, (stadium lights).

Main body text set in Eurostile LT Pro 12/18. Typeface provided by Linotype.